Book Eight

of the

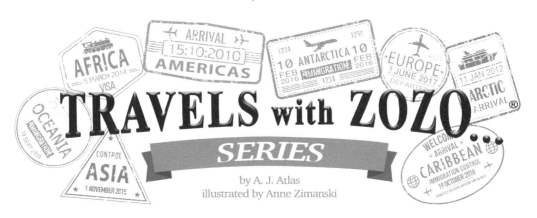

by A. J. Atlas
illustrated by Anne Zimanski

Welcome, Readers!

Before you get started, I thought you might like to know a few interesting things about the Travels with Zozo...® *series. First of all, the stories are set in real places, so the illustrations you'll see try to show the actual landscapes, plants, and animals found in those locations. Second, the scientific, cultural, and historical elements you'll read about are also as accurate as possible. I hope this knowledge makes the books even more enjoyable for you.*

For this story, the setting is Cerro Catedral mountain in the Patagonia region of the Andes Mountain range in South America. The mountain's ski slopes overlook the large Lake Nahuel Huapi (pronounced nah-WELL WAH-pee) and nearby city of San Carlos de Bariloche, usually known as Bariloche (pronounced bah-ree-LOH-cheh), in the country of Argentina. The area is approximately 25-30 miles (40-50 kilometers) from the border between Argentina and Chile.

In a few parts of the story, a teeny bit more creativity and imagination was added. Most of it will be quite obvious, like the skilled, young scouts and their funny, less-than-expert leader. (I think the leader's sagging tent is hilarious and hope you do too!) Other, less obvious, elements that are not 100% accurate include the following:

- *The flags of Argentina and Chile were placed in the illustrations in a general way in order to show that Chile is to the west of Argentina.*

- *Skiing and snowboarding are common activities on Cerro Catedral mountain. Tobogganing, tubing, sledding, and riding flying saucers are not typical.*

- *Foxes should not be approached, even though Zozo does. It is not safe to go near or try to touch unknown animals.*

For the most part, the rest of the information I have presented is accurate and, in my opinion, super interesting! Here are a few more fun facts:

- *Snowflakes form in clouds when water freezes into tiny ice crystals and then the crystals stick together. All snowflakes have six sides, yet no two snowflakes are ever the same. If enough crystals stick together, they will become heavy enough to fall to the ground as snow.*

- *The Andes is the longest above-water mountain range in the world. It is approximately 5,500 miles (8,900 kilometers) long. It extends from south to north through seven South American countries: Argentina, Chile, Bolivia, Peru, Ecuador, Colombia, and Venezuela.*

- *Many different types of animals live in the Andes. This book contains illustrations of some of our favorites, including the guanaco, chinchilla, huemel deer, tuco-tuco, puma, Andean mountain cat, culpeo or Andean fox, Magellanic horned owl, Austral pygmy owl, Patagonian hare or mara, Andean woodpecker, Andean condor, and Andean duck.*

— AJA

TRAVELS with ZOZO®
in the Snow

by A. J. Atlas
illustrated by Anne Zimanski

IMAGINON
BOOKS

Zozo was a

hoppity, floppity,

huggable, snuggable

pet bunny who **loved** to sleep.

She lived with a fun, on-the-run family of four who
loved to travel. Together, they crisscrossed the world
sharing adventures and making new friends.

Zozo and her family were on their first winter vacation.
They arrived very late at night at a cabin in the mountains.
After unpacking and settling in, they went to sleep and
dreamed of the fun that they would have in the days
ahead, skiing, skating, and sledding.

As they slept, clouds drifted in and dropped sparkling, white snow everywhere, making it so that all their dreams could come true.

Just before dawn, Zozo was the first to wake up and
see the wintery wonderland outside. Though she had
seen snow from a distance, she had never seen the icy
crystals up close.

Immediately, she scampered out from under her warm covers and raced to the windows. One window was cracked open, so she leaned out into the cool, crisp air.

"Amazing!" she whispered to the falling snowflakes.

Overwhelmed with curiosity, Zozo leapt out the opened window into the snowbank below. For the first time in her life, she felt gently falling snow on her tail, ears, and whiskers and mounds of it beneath her feet.

"Can I catch a snowflake in my mouth?" she asked herself.
Zozo lifted her nose and opened her mouth. Hopping up,
she caught one, two, three snowflakes on her tongue.
Each one gave a brief, cold tingle before melting.

Leaping and twirling, Zozo flew through the air. Each
time, she landed in the powdery snow for only an instant
before jumping up again.

On one strong jump, Zozo's tongue caught more snowflakes than she could count. But instead of landing softly in the snow, she landed with a thump and felt herself sliding. "Oops!" she cried.

Zozo was on a piece of hard plastic. Shaped like a shallow bowl, it was slippery and moved quickly over the snow.

Zozo zipped rapidly down the steep mountain slope. Though she was scared she might hurt herself if she tried to jump off, she also felt a rush of excitement and wonder.

Down, down, down the mountain, Zozo went, gliding around trees and rocks. "Yippee!" she cheered when she flew through the air after hitting big bumps on the slope.

Halfway down the mountain, the snow
stopped falling. The star-filled sky began
giving way to the oranges, pinks, and
reds of the early morning sunrise.

"I need to stop this saucer and get back up
to my family before they wake up," Zozo told
herself. "But how?"

Suddenly, Zozo's saucer hit another bump in the snow. It flew through the air and landed on top of a clump of bushes. The happy accident had made the saucer finally stop!

Quickly, Zozo slid onto the ground and began climbing as best she could up the mountain in the direction of the cabin.

Hop, hop...whish. Zozo took a few big bounces in the deep snow but then lost her footing and slid back down. *Hop, hop...whish.* Over and over, she tried, only to slide back down.

"This is hard work," she sighed aloud, feeling frustrated and tired. "How will I ever get up this mountain?"

"I happen to know another way," said a voice. Zozo turned to see a young, brown fox peeking out from the bushes beneath the saucer. Using her paws, the fox poked the saucer and shook some branches. With one final tug, she dislodged the saucer from the bushes.

"We will need to go down the mountain a bit more," the fox continued. "Then we can go up with ease." She grinned widely and motioned for Zozo to join her on the saucer.

Zozo didn't understand how they could go up by going down. She did know another saucer ride would be fun, especially with a friend.

Zozo jumped on, and off they went.

"Wheeeee!" the two cheered as they whizzed over the snow, leaning left and right to steer as the fox pointed the way.

Several minutes later, they glided out into a vast clearing. Above them hung benches strung together on a long wire. The wire stretched up the mountain. "Would you like to go for a ride on that chairlift?" the fox asked. "It's the fastest way up."

"Yes!" Zozo agreed.

After landing the saucer in another clump of bushes,
Zozo and the fox darted toward the hanging benches.

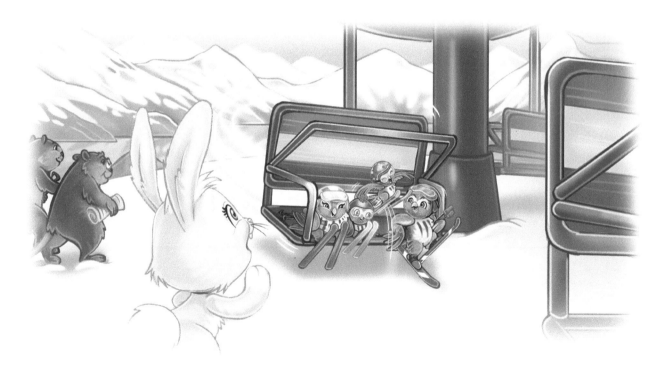

Zozo watched the movement of the benches.
Each moved down the mountain, rounded past
the last pole with a swoosh, and turned upward.

With only a little hesitation and two well-timed hops,
Zozo was soon onboard right beside her new friend.
They were on their way up the mountain!

The ride took them high above the ground where they could see far into the distance. Zozo and the fox stared at the deep lake nearby and the many giant, jagged mountain peaks that surrounded them.

"Patagonia is the home of the Andes," the fox said, motioning proudly with her paw, "the longest chain of mountains in the world!"

Zozo smiled and nodded while looking all around. She saw a beautiful land filled with shimmering water, snow-flocked trees, and animals playing everywhere.

Nearing the mountaintop, Zozo saw the cabin where her family was and felt relieved. At the rounding swoosh of the chairlift, she and the fox took a deep breath and jumped.

They landed with several big rolls. Covered head-to-tail
in snow, they giggled and squirmed to their feet. For Zozo,
everything about the snow felt wonderful.

The fox walked with Zozo to the cabin's open window.
Then the fox picked up another nearby saucer, winked,
and jumped on.

Zozo waved goodbye to the fox and found her way inside,
excited for a snow-filled day of fun with her family.

Discover the colorful northern lights
in Zozo's next adventure,
Travels with Zozo...under the Night Sky!

Travels with Zozo...in the Snow   by A.J. Atlas   illustrated by Anne Zimanski

Published by ImaginOn Books,
an imprint of ImaginOn LLC
www.imaginonbooks.com

Copyright © 2024
by A.J. Atlas

1st Edition
2 4 6 8 10 9 7 5 3 1

Printed
in U.S.A.

978-1-954405-08-0 (Hardcover)   978-1-954405-38-7 (Ebook)

To purchase books or obtain more information about the author, illustrator, or upcoming books,
visit www.travelswithzozo.com

Printed in the USA
CPSIA information can be obtained
at www.ICGtesting.com
JSHW040343150224
56971JS00007B/6